Smaragdi Mitropoulou

One Moment, Just an Eternity

Translation:

Katherine Reilly

Pharos Books

ISBN: 978-93-5546-122-3
eISBN: 978-93-5546-130-8

©Publisher

Publisher: Pharos Books (P) Ltd.
Plot No.-55, Main Mother Dairy Road
Pandav Nagar, East Delhi-110092
Phone: 011-40395855, +14049995474
WhatsApp: +91 8368220032
E-mail: sales@pharosbooks.in
Website: www.pharosbooks.in
First Edition: 2022

Printed By: Sushma Book Binding House, Okhla
Industrial Area, Phase II, New Delhi-11002

ONE MOMENT JUST AN ETERNITY
SMARAGDI MITROPOULOU

To you, my sun and master.

You've risen over the stars, but you're next to me driving

my mind, my soul and my pen.

Introduction

Theophanes L. Panayotopoulos

"One moment, just an eternity." At first the title sounds peculiar, but behind there is a riddle. Can a moment last for an eternity?

This book consists of two parts:

The first part is a little novel, where the author in a masterly way marries the West with the Oriental element. Sometimes it wraps a turban around our forehead and travels us under the warm desert sun and around the oasis El Hena and sometimes cools us down in the blue-green Aegean. It whispers to us about the princess of the East who transforms souls into singing flowers and then tells us about the admirable grace of the Holy Mary. And all this under the sounds of a gypsy violin.

The second part consists of eight separate stories. We are introduced to Ayse, who allures us to an invisible dance with her. It tells us about the dreams that have become dust. It travels us to a sea of memories. And then it tells us Shehrazade's story, taking us into another world.

Human weaknesses, love, hopelessness, passion, friendship, dreams and expectations are some of the issues that the author is dealing with, even giving them social implications.

I insist on another world. I've dreamed of it so much, so much I've perambulated inside of it so as now it is impossible not to exist, poet Christos Laskaris once wrote.

That's exactly how we perambulate the magic world of Smaragdi Mitropoulou.

Theophanes L. Panayotopoulos is a the ologist, poet, author and radio producer

PART Aʹ

ONE MOMENT, JUST AN ETERNITY

A mark can last forever and a moment to mark the soul for an eternity

2014 Fantastic Larry Niven Literature Award

Contents

One moment, just an eternity

My heart travels to the Aegean.

Once upon a time on a blessed island

floodlighted by the grace of the Holy Mary...

A building as white as a dove, clambered on the rock gazing at the sea, a gate rusty from the slurry, a garden full of weeds: this is my new world.

And then...

I see you standing discreet on a side, a diminutive creature with the sweetest eyes in the world, and I feel my heart breaking into millions of pieces. I loved you even before I knew your name. One moment was enough to bring my being upside down.

One moment, just an eternity.

How can the sky suddenly darken? I'm approaching you and you're avoiding me. You put your little hands on your little head like you want to protect it from something. *From me??? Why are you afraid of me?* I... I would give my life for you.

I asked and learned. How much have you been hurt, my sweetheart. Threats, bad words, beating.

By what right? I wonder.

A dark endless night, a night of Thursday dawning Friday. It was raining and lightning outside. And I was writing and tearing up. I was smoking one cigarette after the other, the cup of coffee next to me had long been cold. My whole being was one tear, my soul was bleeding.

Just one moment, a goddamn moment, was enough to make you look at me like a scared little animal. I wanted to yell out loud: *I love you, what scares you?* But it was like the voice had stumbled somewhere and never come out.

 You cringe and tremble when I approach you, your sad look a knife in my heart.

Show strength, my lad, strength! I'm whispering to you.

Can you hear me, my sweetheart? Do you hear me?

Our life is a sea, my eyes, sometimes rough and sometimes peaceful. Don't yield, stand on your feet. **I LOVE YOU!!** How could I betray you? It'd be like dying twice.

I'll never let anyone hurt you again and I will pay any price, if necessary. As long as *you* are all right, you who still didn't have the time to dream.

Time is the best healer. Little by little your smile is coming back. However...

A bite in the heart, a strange presage. I can't rest. I feel like *something* is going to happen...

I run the gauntlet from everywhere. You also want to protect me. Don't bear that burden on your soul. This is my debt.

I'm a big girl, I'm telling you. You can't forbid me to love you and protect you, you answer me.

After a while, your eyes get a dreamy look.

"What color is the smile?" you ask me.

"The blue of the sky and the sea," I answer.

And you open your little hands and lock me in. If you knew how much I needed that!

"And the evil? How is the evil?" you numbly ask me again. What can I answer? It has, you see, too many and weird forms. Faces dry enough to deplete their severity on an innocent and weak creature, bitter words, a demeaning gaze, cruel, like poison.

"I'm afraid for you," you tell me.
"What are you afraid of, honey? Everything is fine," I'm trying to assure you.
"Is it?"
You look at me with a little distrust.
A few feet away, evil lurks. A murder weapon, a finger that pulls the trigger...
I have to run!
Fire...
I have to make it!
A white shirt is stained red.
A blur.
Silence.

It's getting dark, I'm scared. Hold my hand. I whisper your name over and over again until my heart counts her last beat. Tonight my soul, sitting on a white cloud, flies over the Aegean. And you sit in our favorite corner and look at the horizon like you're looking for something... someone. Do you see me, my eyes? Here I am, next to you, I will never abandon you... never... never...

Like a wind I'm passing by leaving a caress on your hair. You bring your finger to the lips and send a kiss that comes and lands on my eyes.

I smile, and then I get lost.
One moment, just an eternity.
Done.
Or maybe a new beginning?
I love you... you remember that.

Witch of the stars

I stood by the hours gazing the sea. My eyes were looking at the horizon as if they were looking for something... someone. And always before me the same image: a white shirt painted red, a smile that froze. And I held her hand tight just before the end, just before her soul started the journey for the land where stars never set.

One moment, just an eternity, was enough to bring my whole being upside down! As soon as our eyes crossed, that day I first saw her, I knew... yes... I knew.

"Witch of the stars," I called her.

She had a rare ability to read the secrets of the human soul, and her heart looked so much like ours, like of the children's she had sworn to love and protect.

***

It has got dark long ago. The stars are shining in the sky. Everybody's asleep, but I'm awake. Light steps make me turn my head. It's my spiritual, Father Gabriel. He sits next to me.

"If it weren't for me, she would still be alive!" I broke the silence first.

"It's not your fault! She loved you so much, that she chose to leave!"

I gently caressed the little silver crucifix I kept carefully in my pocket. At one side it was stained with blood.

"She never parted with it... and gave it to me, just the moment before!!! There's her blood..." sobs are shaking my body, they don't let me go on.

I jump up on my feet.

"Where are you going?"
I pause for a moment.
"To find redemption!"
And I'm wending my way.

***

My room is my hideaway, which hosts my own secrets. I pull out of my closet a big box and I open it with shaking hands. Instantly the smell of dried roses floods the space.

How many things are locked in there: drawings with smiling flowers and shining stars, a few illustrated books that traveled me to the world of fairy tales and dreams. I close my eyes and I think I hear her voice: Once upon a time... and they lived happily ever after.....life itself is the most beautiful fairy tale... Among them a black, leather file. My eyes are misting over. I remember...

While my witch was looking at the Throne of Holy Mary, I was approached by an elderly gentleman. With just one look at him, I understood. The resemblance was amazing! Especially the smile and the pervasive stare, which concealed such love and kindness, behind its grief.

"This is for you!" he told me and put it in my hands.

I looked at him wondering.

"What's in it?" I asked him.

"You will see!" he told me, avoiding giving me a direct answer.

"Just... open it when you feel ready!"

"Why me?"

"There is no why! Hold it!"

Just like that, he was gone.
I never saw him again.
I gently drag my fingers on its surface and I browse it. I'm ready to open it, but I hesitate. *Am I ready, really? … I* wonder. I take those thoughts out of my mind, and take a deep breath...
A whole world springs from inside, her world. Fairy tales, short stories, plays... the unfolding of her soul. And among them — *oh, my God!* — that novel of hers, whose content she kept as a guarded secret.
"Won't you give it to us to read it?" we asked her, pressingly sometimes.
She was smiling.
"It's a secret!" she was only telling us. "Until when??" we were asking again.
"Oh, you're too inquisitive!" she was shouting almost angry. Only that her anger lasted a little. And now everything is right in front of me. All her character make-up, captured on paper.
Suddenly I push everything aside and burst into tears. Why? Why?... I hit the pillow with my fists over and over again.
One hand is touching my head affectionately.
"Witch of the stars!" I whisper.
 "It's me, my boy!" Father-Gabriel's voice brings me back to reality.
"See what's left now ... a stack of papers! Just that...!!" I say while trembling.
"Among them there's something left of her, my boy. Her words, her soul, her heart... all her heartbeats laid in here... "
He wipes my eyes with a tissue.

"But if it hurts you so much... they're yours now... you can do whatever you want, even throw them away..."

I shudder even at hearing it.

"Never! Never!" I say. *"This will never happen!"*

"Fight, my boy! Go ahead! Strength, my dear! Don't let her sacrifice go in vain!"

Strength, my dear, strength... those words of her, my shield. The sound of the bell, which is ringing for the evening Mass, puts an end to our conversation. I beg him-only for tonight-not to accompany him. He accepts. He crosses my forehead with his hand and leaves.

I open the first page and...

A flower was born tonight

violinists play songs for love.

The moon smiled tonight.

Her eyes nodded me

an arrow on my chest.

A gypsy witch

tonight took my heart.

A witch of the stars!

I'm reading it again and again. The lyrics are hers, the most beautiful beginning for a story. I sense that it's going to travel me. I sit more comfortably on my bed, putting a pillow under my back. Tonight the night will be long...

***

It's almost dawn when I close the last page...
Tonight I hugged a moon.
Marks of the moon on my chest how
much I loved you, gypsy witch.

A journey along the paths of the Middle Ages, through ruined castles, through Byzantine iconography, through the tear of the gypsy violin for a love that never died out.

I raise my eyes to the sky. The stars are starting to set, but a big star, the brightest, still shines.

Really, how was that fairy tale from the East? Oh, yeah! The souls of those we love become night stars that shine on the empyrean and during the day they travel upon a white cloud.

I open my room door and slip out. I go and sit at my favorite spot. I know that her soul will fly over the Aegean and come to find me. It's calm today, leaves don't move. Yet... a soft breeze strokes my head. I know. I bring my finger to the lips and send a kiss.

"I love you, remember that!"... a whisper in my ears... and the voice so familiar.

I extend my arms open wide.

"I love you, remember that!" I yell out loud which sounds like an echo in the quietness of the morning.

It is now dawn over the Aegean.

Tamra Hena

The sky, all of a sudden, was filled with stardust.

Where am I? Where am I going?

I float between yesterday, today and tomorrow.

I started on a white cloud, flying over the Aegean. Just one word: *"I love you, remember that"*... and then I was lost in the heights, looking for a new homeland. A rider on a red stallion held my hand and led me here, to the East. Its myths say that souls become stars that shine on the empyrean. But, they can start living all over again. *Is that possible?*

The stardust is increasing... increasing... increasing.... it's falling down to earth and slowly takes form...

*****

Somewhere in the hot desert, the oasis El Hena rests the eye of every tired wayfarer, quenches his dried lips, gives him strength to continue. Its residents live simply, tidily and praise Allah daily for the precious gift of life.

Among them a strange woman, with brown almond-shaped eyes and red hair. She lives with them, giving them her smile freely, because they embraced her with love, when she arrived there on a rainy night, at the brink of exhaustion. Three days and nights she was burning with fever and she was in delirium, strange words which were quickly forgotten. When she recovered, she begged them to start a big fire... there she threw away the clothes she was wearing, sat down and watched the flames that went up high. Now she wears clothes woven from their hands, as if she were theirs ever since she was born. She gets up first, goes to the spring to bring water, and sometimes, when she's alone, she lets a song escape her lips which talks about violins and moons.

***

I sing during night hours, when the stars shine above the desert sky. It's hot tonight. I approach the river, leaving my clothes on the bank and dive into the waters naked. Its arms are cool, soft is its caress.

I'm not alone…

Behind a palm tree, I feel like someone's watching me. I'm holding my breath.

"Who's there?" I'm about to yell, but the voice doesn't come out.

I hear footsteps. I turn my head around and the first thing I see is two eyes, your eyes. You're getting close. You are taking off your clothes and dive into the water.

You're coming close to me. I feel your gaze stroking me.

You reach out your hand to me, you hug me.

My heart beats fast!

"Tamra Hena!" you whisper, while we lie on the ground and your body becomes one with mine.

Gently, sweetly, tenderly, like the breeze that blows between the palm trees, but also wildly, violently, like the water of the river, you lead me to the paths of happiness, you drip inside me the sweetest wine, and I want to drink it to the end, to drain the last drop, before it's too late and the dream is over.

As the new day dawns, the first thing I see is a strange flower on my bedside with a heady perfume. Its name? Tamra Hena.

"Tamra Hena... for me!" you tell me.

Yeah, for you, I'm thinking and I'm leaning over you. Who cares about yesterday or tomorrow? It's enough that you're here now...

Tamra Hena, then.

In a moment... and a light opens my ways.

One moment was enough to love you deeply, strongly, absolutely.

One moment, just an eternity.

And time flies like the waters of the river.

Tamra Hena...

Now my clothes have the blue color of the sky, a sweet color that softens the red fire of my hair.

"A fire I want to burn me to eternity ... your eyes, stars of heaven, Tamra Hena!" you whisper to me.

***

The desert sky is strange tonight, strange are its marks.

Why, really? A strong wind is blowing...

"Orestes!" I whisper unconsciously.

Where does that name come from?

And then... I see stardust falling from above... and approaching me...

An image flashes in my mind: Once, in a previous life, they called me *"witch of the stars"*. And a lot more other images start passing in front of me...

Something tells me I need to travel again. The same hand that led me here, now is showing me that it's time...

"Until when?" I whisper to the rider as I climb up the red stallion. He's not answering me.

"Until when?" I ask again.

"Your heart will tell you..." His voice is deep and impressive.

We go up high, the stardust hugs us...

***

A building as white as a dove, clambered on the rock gazing at the sea, a gate rusty from the slurry, a garden full of weeds...

"Here again?" my voice trembles.

"This is where you testified your soul, remember?" says the rider.

"She belongs elsewhere now!" I say, almost with anger. *"I don't want to see..."*

"You make your presence felt in any way you want now, witch of the stars! As for the rest, the road will always be open, as long as you won't get your blue dress dirty," he says darkly and disappears.

A form from flesh and blood that no one can see. Crying, yelling... and a child's soul is bleeding.

"You cannot, you do not have the right!" his voice, my little sparrow's voice.

The one whose hand pulled the trigger at that time, is trying to take from him by force something he holds tight on his chest.

I freeze. It's a drawing of smiling flowers and shining stars......

Finally, she grabs it from his hands, shreds it and throws it into the waste bin. I'm tightening my fists. I see her coming out of the hall. I'm following her. She goes and sits in a corner, lights up a cigarette.

She doesn't see me. It's too easy to push her and throw her off the ledge. Who would suspect? An accident, everyone will say.

I'm taking a step towards her...

"The road will always be open, as long as you won't get your blue dress dirty!" the rider's voice.

"Tamra Hena, witch of the stars"... my heart beats fast. It's not worth it... she's not worth it losing the desert wind, the palms of El Hena oasis... and especially him...!! Let it be forgotten, I think.

My crying little sparrow is trying to assemble the torn drawing, when suddenly a strong wind opens the window of the hall and a beautiful flower, with a heady perfume, lands on his feet. He takes it in his hands, he touches it on his cheek...

Tamra Hena.

***

I open my eyes and see the palm trees and the crystal clear waters of the river. *Was I dreaming?*

I'm wearing my blue dress, but there's a suspicion of stardust on it.

"My darling...Tamra Hena!" the voice of my sweetheart is balm, sweeter than honey.

Tamra Henna, means flower. *Tamra Hena*, means sensuous perfume. *Tamra Hena*, means love.

Beneath the desert sky, between the palm trees and next to the gargling waters of the oasis El Hena, in one moment I met my own destiny, *my kismet*, which will last for an eternity.

The road will always be open...

In the courtyard of that white building that's clambered on the rock,
grew a flower that can't be found elsewhere in the area. Its petals
are a combination of white and red, its perfume is wonderful…
And when it's beginning to dawn, there's a whisper like a song:

A flower was born tonight.
Play, oh play songs, violinist, for love.

Scent of the East overlooking the Aegean.

Princess of the East

Everything is desolated.

The white building was left all alone on the rock, it laments while looking at the sea and the seagulls, desperately waiting for something... someone..

The sky darkened. The blessed island – *which was floodlighted by the Holy Mother's mercy* - was in pain.

> *A cry of agony by innocent souls:*
> *Don't let them imprison our heart.*
> *Don't let us be condemned to mental orphanhood.*
> *Don't let them steal our dream.*

Silence. Everything seemed dead.

But...

The strange plant was still there, blooming and scenting. It has been growing ever since one autumn night, getting stronger and stronger. It was a gorgeous flower whose fragrance paralyzed the senses, white as purity and red as passion.

Various stories were linked to its existence. Some were talking about a killing, about a strange presence-invisible but very real-and about a song.

Who can confirm them? Those who had a share of responsibility, had spread like leaves in the wind, had sunk into oblivion.

Except for...

***

On the other side of the Aegean, in the place where the greatest Apocalypse of all centuries took place, I chose to lay down my hurt soul. The dried petals of a flower that once landed on my feet and a box full of manuscripts and drawings are my most precious treasures. During the hours of solitude and contemplation, especially when the night falls, my mind is filled with her, my witch. And then I take a notebook and I write and erase... I write and erase.

Words that come straight from the heart... thoughts ill-assorted and confused... but they're only for me... that become one with my dreams... as if living them...

***

The woman in the blue dress left her goblet with water next to her and let her eyes gaze beyond the horizon. Time here was passing by slowly... calmly... like the blessed waters of the river that gave life to El Hena oasis. The nights were filled with songs and sounds of the timbale under the desert sky. Like tonight.

> *Oh Tamra Hena come back*
> *Do you hear your beloved calling you?*
> *The flowers of our garden have wilted*
> *only you can raise them up*
> *with one of your touch, Tamra Hena.*

She smiled at the sound of the singing voice. It was her beloved, the light of her life...!!

She sleeked her hair a little, and in quick steps, she went there where the others were gathered, by the river. The fires they had lit were strong, almost like daylight. The rhythm tempted her to dance. So, she started to sway her body with grace, while the sound of the timbale was getting stronger and stronger.

*Your eyes black like the charcoal burning in the
fire your lips red like ripe cherries Oh Tamra Hena,
lady of my heart Oh Tamra Hena, Princess of the East...*

***

All around me a scent... similar to that... then...! In my ears, the echo of music from percussion instruments while in front of me the same image passing: a woman with long red hair dancing under the moonlight. Her moves, her smile, her eyes, as they are set on mine.......!! And that song...

I finally had her in front of me!! She once taught me how to spell the stars alphabet. She was the witch of the stars, the princess of the east, my witch!

Just for one moment!!! And then everything was gone and I found myself alone in my little room.

At the same time the sound of the bell was heard, which called us for the day's lessons.

So it was just a vision? Product of my imagination? I thought looking for the clothes I had to wear.

But how??? My thought was abruptly interrupted.

On my bedside table there was a flower, identical to that old one...!

I take it in my hands, I touch it on my cheek.

"You are close to me ... you are close to me!!!" I whisper.

A discreet knock on the door gave me a start.

"Orestes, are you ready? Don't be late!" I hear the voice of one of my classmates.

I am about to turn the key and open the door, but I regret it.

"I... I can't...", I'm stumbling. *"I'm not well ... my stomach ... it hurts!"* How easily I let drop the lie... even half a lie! But, seriously, I have no strength left. I want to stay with my thoughts.

I snuggle under the bed covers, I hide the flower in my arms and I suck its scent. In the hallway, my classmates' footsteps are heard. Little by little they fade away.

I put my hand on my bedside and I pull out my favorite notebook. Slowly, carefully I turn its pages. Then I take a pencil and I start writing what I've lived through the dream last night. I'm in a strange hurry... I'm in need to protect my secrets.

***

A strong wind was blowing between the palm trees, while a gray dull color covered the desert sky. The residents of El Hena oasis were locked in their little houses, flinching in the corners out of fear. Only Tamra Hena understood the signs. It was time.

"Will you travel again? There?" her beloved asked her, tangling his fingers in her hair.

"Can't you hear?" she told him.

There were sounds of horse-riding, which, as the hour passed, became stronger and stronger.

How long has it been since that last trip? She didn't even remember. After all, she no longer had to count time.

The horseman with the red stallion stood in front of her and extended his hand.

"Come on!" he simply told her.

"I thought that...", she mumbled.

"Come!" he told her again imperatively.

She obeyed.

They went up high, a cloud of stardust covered them.

The young man followed them with his eyes.

"You will come back here again, to me, to us!! Like back then! Like always! Now I know, my darling. And I'm no longer afraid of losing you," he said in a low voice knowing that his words touched her heart.

***

I fill a paper cup with water and put the flower in. I'm caressing it. I bend over and kiss its petals. A whisper sounds in my ears...

The moon smiled tonight...

I let out a loud cry of joy. Then another... and another...and another...

Suddenly I feel a strong tingle on my cheek!

***

Tamra Hena let out gasp of pain.

"He was hit in the face," said the horseman.

She shook her head and looked around. Above them the vast blue sky, beneath the vast blue of the Aegean. A boat was shearing through the calm water. Go...

***

Master Emilian carefully thumbs through the notebook he holds in his hands. The puzzlement is pervasive on his face. Next to him is Miss Julita. The traces of her fingers imprinted on my cheek... her words as an echo ring in my ears.

"He must be severely punished, Mr Principal!"

Looks like the past still haunts me. Her best friend (whose name I don't even stand to say!), who back then turned my life upside down, had just taken over here. Oh, my God! I'm thinking.

She was teaching us, I remember, literature and history. Formally, as she was supposed to do. Nothing less, nothing more. I don't blame her, she taught us a lot of useful things: names, dates, figures of speech. As she was supposed to do!

An empty look and lips always ripply! No comparison to my witch's broth and flame! But not all people are the same, as Father Gabriel said. That way we could coexist...

"I will deal with this, Miss Julita!" the voice of Master Emilian brings me back to the present.

She is ready to say something, but he cuts it with a nod.

"You can go!" he says.

I'm giving her, as she leaves, a hostile look, but one that doesn't escape my principal's watchful eye.

He closes the door, takes a chair and sits next to me.

"I think that belongs to you," he says, and leaves the notebook in front of me.

"Thank you!" I say with a voice which is barely heard. I take it and clasp it on me.

"Well?" he asks me, while he grabs my chin and makes me lift my head.

A tear runs down my cheek. He pretends he doesn't see it.

Don't lower your eyes, my soul... her voice. Even when you have to apologize for something, you will do it by looking the other one in the eye.

"Well?" he asks me again.

"Well, you know..."

I'm caressing the notebook unawarely.

The wave in my chest is growing... growing... and it's asking to be thrown out.

You can trust me…, his voice embrangles with hers.

So I start talking... and talking... without stopping, breathlessly... about everything.

A soft scent hits the nostrils, which, as the time passes, gets stronger.

I look master Emilian straight in the eye.

"Do you feel it? It's here! It's everywhere!" I whisper.

He smiled and stroked my head.

***

It was far into the night, but a strange glow was illuminating the devastated building, as if a lot of stars were falling altogether in its backyard, while a sweet, whispering sound filled the air.

No one realized it, except for the little boy who had just come off the ship. His heart was beating fast as he was stepping on the ground that he'd loved so much...

"Do you hear it, Mr. Giannis?" he nudged the tall man who accompanied him.

"What, my Orestes?"

"The music! The song!"

He floundered.

"I ... I don't hear ... anything!" he said.

But the child insisted.

"And yet ... I'm sure you can hear it ..." he underlined his words one by one.

Mr. Giannis tried to smile. He was a music teacher, for many years, telling his students that sounds are inside us...they're just waiting for the right stimulus, the right moment to come out.

And now, a phone call from his old school principal made him leave his job and obligations and make that long journey to his hometown, to escort this little boy to the island of Holy Mary.

"Only you can stand next to him ... to see ... to listen ...!" Emilian told him, after he had recounted to him the events in detail.

"Why only me?" he wondered.

"Because you have a pure soul just like a child, my Giannis, despite the years that weigh on your back!"

"I'm sure you can hear it!" Orestes said again.

"Maybe... we'll... we'll see..."

"Let's go!" The kid caught him by the hand and started climbing the alley.

***

The stardust falls on the earth taking shape and form. Tamra Hena roamed for some time alone in the landscape of her previous life. It's all the same, but all so different at the same time.

The church clock schemed once... twice... It's almost time... it's almost time... the horseman's words.

A strange shiver went through her body.

The church clock kept scheming...

***

The church clock is scheming hard...
Three times... four times... five times...
It's following my heartbeat.
And we're getting closer... and closer... and closer. There is a thick chain with a lock around the iron door. "How are we going to get in?" asks Mr Giannis, waving his head in despair.
"We will jump over the bars..."
He looks at me surprised.
 "Are you afraid?" I ask him with a hidden irony.
"No... no... of course not..."
His embarrassment is obvious.
"Let's go, then..."
The church clock keeps scheming...
Six times... seven times... eight times...
The light is getting brighter.
We enter the courtyard.
Nine times... ten times...
In front of us the beloved flower...
 Mr Giannis is slightly blanched.
"It's ... it's so beautiful!" he says with a voice that can barely be heard.
Eleven times...
An exquisite scent fills the space...
Mr. Giannis breathes deep. I'm smiling at him.
Twelve times!!
Midnight!!
The light suddenly became brighter, as if it were daytime. The leaves and flowers swayed slightly. A woman with long red hair,

dressed in light blue, and a man dragging from the reins a horse with red fur, appeared before us...

"My witch..." I whisper.

I run to her, I hug her, I clasp her on me. No, I'm not dreaming this time! She's here, near me!

Mr. Giannis' legs are stuck on the ground. I beckon him. He approaches with trembling steps. He's staring at her in the eyes.

"You?" he only says.

She's reaching out to him. He grabs her hand and tightens it in his two hands. He makes sure he touches a shape of flesh and blood.. even if...

"The flower ... the scent ... the light ..." he whispers.

"Nothing was a lie!" she responds.

"Where is the truth?" he asks.

The rider approached us and made a move, as if he was opening an invisible curtain...

***

She was going up and down full of anger, smoking one cigarette after the other. Her gaze was like poison.

"He won't be cured ... no ... he won't," she mumbled. *"Who does he think he is? How dare he?"*

In the next office, someone was whispering, yet intensely, on the phone. After a while the sound of the headphone was heard, and the door was opened with a bang.

"Mr. Director?" she asked him.

"Don't worry, Lillian, soon things will set in rights!"

He grabbed his head with his two hands. He was in a constant headache with that redheaded colleague of his who *"law unto herself and didn't mean to be confined to her class and only that..."*
"I have to find a way, I have to ...", he mulled...
"You called me?" her warm, kind voice distracted him from his thoughts.
"Yes... we need to talk..."
He closed the door. After a while a fight was heard from inside.
"You're going too far! Watch out!"
"Only dead...did you hear me?????"
She opened the door and left running. She didn't even notice that from the teachers' office the other one was watching her while her eyes were shining strangely... like she was preparing something.

***

To me she was the one who pulled the trigger...! My mind was stubbornly refusing to recognize that she had a name. And yes, she had! It was Evaggelia, whom everyone called Lillian. I have a dry smile! She wasn't even close to 'Evaggelia' (happy Gospel). Her role was more that of the "angel of bad news".
I have a lump in the throat, I feel like I'm going to burst.
But I have to be strong.
Strength... strength..., the words of my witch-whom now I can see and touch- is my shield.

***

It was almost dark. In Orestes' small room there were books all over the place, on his desk, on his bed, even on the floor. Sitting on a chair, the redhead was having a last look at his notebook. The kid had just recovered from the awful cold and the fever that had tortured him over the past few days and the next day he would return to his classes. That's why she had gone — with his teacher's permission — to help him in his studying, so as to fill in whatever blanks there were.

"Do you have another question, maybe?" she asked him. *"No! I understood everything... thanks to my witch!"* he said with pride.

"Young man...!!!!"

"Don't be angry at me..." he complained to her. *"You know that everything I tell you comes from my heart..."*

She smiled, stood up and opened the window blinds. The place was filled with autumn's breeze.

***

Behind the huge palm tree, protected by the half-darkness, the two figures were talking, albeit whispering, but tensely...

"Lillian, for God's sake, what are you doing?" the voice was almost begging.

"Enough! Shut up you, too!"

"But..."

"I know what I'm doing! Shut up..."

***

"Oh, how much I longed to go out a little!" said the kid, going out into the garden. The redhead followed him.

"Young man, be careful, you'll get cold again!" she said. *"I'm fine!"* he replied. *"There, see, I even wore my jacket! But you, you're going to catch a cold going out with the shirt! That humidity will affect you!"*

"Oh, I'm copper-bottomed, don't be afraid!"

The kid stayed still watching her for a few minutes.

"You know... your smile is very beautiful! Never lose your smile! Do you promise me?"

"I promise!"

All of the sudden, his eyes had a dreamy look.

"I wonder ... what color does smile have?" he whispered.

"The blue of the sky and the sea," said the redhead.

Spontaneously, the kid opened his hands and hugged her.

"I love you very much!" he told her.

"Me too, my eyes!" she said, touched with emotion.

"And... and evil... what's evil like?" he asked her again numbly.

The redhead grew a bit pale.

"It has ... it has so many forms ... don't ... don't ask me for an answer," she said quietly.

"I'm afraid… for you..."

"What are you afraid of, honey? Everything is fine."

The little guy looked at her with a little distrust. No, nothing was fine. He knew that his witch (as he called the redhead) had been through many difficult times since she stood beside him and took him under her wing. Really, how blind some people were... how blind!

"Is it?" he insisted.

"Yes... it is..." she tried to assure him.

***

Lillian put her hand in the pocket and took it out with precaution...
"Where did you find it???" the other one asked her with saucer eyes.
"Don't ask..."
"Let's go..." she begged her. *"I cannot ... I cannot ..."*
She grabbed her friend from the arm and touched the barrel of the gun she was holding on her chest.
"Too bad, Julita! And I thought you were willing to help me..."
"Not for that! Oh please don't!!!"
Always pushing the gun on her, Lillian pulled her closer to her and started whispering in her ear... telling her... and telling her… Julita shuddered...
"Well?"
Julita nodded *"yes"* with the head, shaking.
"I want to hear it from your lips!" the other one insisted. *"I ... will do whatever you say!"* she said, while her teeth were beating.
"Go there!" she showed her a spot across theirs. *"And... close your eyes and ears, okay?"*
"Uh... okay!"

***

"Let's go inside, it's cold ..." said the kid by pulling the redhead from her hand.

The sound of steps on the dry grass made her pause.
"Who's there?" she yelled.
"Let's go inside! There is nothing..."
The voice froze in his throat, as he saw the gun pointing at him and a pair of eyes, frozen and glassy, staring at him. Terror paralyzed him...
The finger pulled the trigger. A loud cry was heard:
"NOOOOOOOOO!!!"
With a salto, Lillian was lost in the dark.
The lights in the chambers were turned on, some kids rushed outside.
"What happened? How did it happen?" they shouted.
They didn't hear anything.
The little boy didn't answer. For him time stopped abruptly as his witch stormed between him and the gat and then fell down! A blood stain was formed on her chest that it grew bigger... and bigger... and bigger... painting red her white shirt.
Someone called for an ambulance.
The redhead moved her lips slowly. The child kneeled near her.
"Hold on, girl, it's going to be okay! Strength! Strength!" he shouted grabbing her hand.
"I'm scared!" she mumbled.
"I am here ... strength ... strength ...", he continued telling her.
"It's getting dark ... I'm afraid ... don't leave me!!"
"Here I am...! Here!!'

"Don't... don't... forget me... Orestes... my little Orestes..." and with those words, she died.

***

Lillian unlocked her apartment door and went in. She slowly took off the gloves she was wearing, and a smirking smile was formed on her face. Everything went just fine! She had made sure not to leave traces anywhere, the gun and the silencer were now in the wet embrace of the sea, and — mostly — *SHE* no longer existed.

 "You're awesome!" she said to her idol mirroring on the hall mirror. *"You were right to turn the gun against him! It was easy to guess...! SHE would even give her life for the kid!! Finally, you didn't go wrong!"*
Nobody heard anything... nobody saw anything...! She was holding her friend in hand, and as for the child, she wasn't worrying. She knew what she had to do.

***

I let the tears flow freely, hiding my face in the arms of Tamra Hena, my witch. She's trying to calm me down, whispering to me *"I'm here now!"* The rider tells her to let me take it out of me, to relieve myself.
Mr. Giannis with a pasty face, was giving one look at Tamra Henna and one at the dead woman in the bloody shirt. Yeah, it was the same person!
He brought it all back to his mind: the funeral, the old man with the leather folder which now belonged to little Orestes... and especially the revelations made to him by master Emilian, which were recorded in the child's brown leather textbook ... the one which

Miss Julita had accidentally discovered along with the exotic flower and....

She was insistently demanding that he be punished and removed from school - on the accusation of dealing with magic and idolatry (!) – as to cover the tracks of her old friend and hers. She was intended to bring it forward to the Teachers' Association…

Luckily, his old school principal handled the matter properly.

He gently pulled me out of my witch's arms and placed his hand on my shoulder.

"I was the only one who saw what happened ..." I whispered looking him in the eye. *"But..."*

"But? ..."

Words come out of me like a torrent.

"They claimed that ... I had imagined everything... that... I was in delirium because of the fever ... Lillian had spent all night at her house and Julita who was with her confirmed it!!!!! I insisted... I insisted... no one believed me!! The... the Director... asked to close the case because of lack of evidence...!! He... Lillian... Julita... they acted as if my witch never existed… the rest… only on behalf of themselves… and nothing more! But I... I felt her next to me... near me... inside me... around me...! That flower you see... there isn't another one alike in the area... I heard it sing... the hours of dawn... only me... only me!!!!... My only companion!!! My good dear father-Gabriel... they took care of it and removed him from here...!! Slander...slander!! He left...he followed a mission to Africa... to Zaire!! We had no contact anymore!!!!..."

Tamra Henna nodded as if she wanted to confirm my words.

It's the first light of dawn.

"This time..." I whispered and winked to Mr. Giannis.

"Do you believe that...??"
"Yes... I believe..."
Mr. Giannis approaches the flower, touches it and puts his ear on its petals while closing his eyes.
"I believe too... I believe too..." he says in a low voice.
The song is flooding my heart and my friend's ears.
Carved deep the marks of your moon...
How much I loved you, Gypsy witch...
Mr. Giannis laughs like a child! He hugs me and twirls me...
"I heard it! I heard the flower singing! I heard it, yes, I heard it!! It's all true!!" he keeps repeating.
"The gate of light has opened..." said my witch. She stroked my head and kissed me on the forehead.
"I love you, remember that!" she whispers to me. *"I love you too, my witch, my Tamra Hena!"* *"Remember ... the road will always be open!"* the rider intervened.
"Would it be possible ... to take the flower with us?" asks Mr Giannis, making a move to uproot it.
"Leave it! Just take a branch...and plant it where you're going...!" she tells us.
"But, the branch how?"... Mr. Giannis asks again. *"Anything is possible!! As long as you believe it..."* She looked me deep in the eyes.

"Plant it on the earth... just you, my boy, no one else. It's going to grow roots... and the flower will bloom again, on the other side of the Aegean... and wherever your kismet takes you. It will ramble, it will thrive, it will proclaim its existence, so as hope will never fade!"

The rider mounts the horse and winks at her. She follows him.

"Wait, just a moment!" shouts Mr Giannis.

"What doubts still lie in you, man?"

Mr. Giannis bowed his head.

"When... when I was a child... I once saw this same flower in a fairy tale that... that talked about a princess of the East... it was her soul...! I loved that story, it's just that..."

"What?"

"A word at the end was written in a language I didn't know.. and I never learned its meaning ....'

"What was the name? Do you remember?" the rider asked him, spurring with his feet the sides of the horse.

"Maktoub!! What... what does that mean? Perhaps you know to tell me."

"Maktoub means it's written!" the rider shouted.

We sat on the stone bench and watched the red stallion rising up high... and high... and high, until it was lost from our sight, leaving behind a fine line of stardust...

***

I'm gazing the island of Holy Mary as the ship moves away. I hold the little clay pot with the precious branch my witch gave me with her own hands.

So, the East plant with the wonderful scent will continue to exist, to bloom, to ramble and to thrive, while with the first light of dawn the favorite song will be heard:

The moon smiled tonight...

Her eyes nodded me an arrow on my chest...

And I'll listen to it with my soul and add...
A gypsy witch tonight took my heart...
a witch of the stars...
The stardust became one with the sun that had been rising for some time, and then it sank in the waters of the Aegean.

From the daily press...

THESSALONIKI, 10/10…- *In a dry well at the area of Yedi Kule (Old City), the body of Evangelia M. was discovered, aged 36, who had disappeared since last week…*

PATMOS, 10/10….-*On the site of Grikos near "Kallikatsu" rock, Julita K., aged 32, was found dead…*

MYKONOS, 10/10— *Mystery covers the death of 52-year-old Efthymios P, who was found mangled in his apartment…*

According to the investigations, the three dead had been colleagues in the past. Even though their time of death confirmed as 3rd, 5th and 7th morning hours respectively, the hands of their watches had stopped at exactly 12pm!!! Many questions have also aroused by the note found next to each one. It contained exactly the same words: ONE MOMENT, JUST AN ETERNITY, as well as a word with Latin and Greek characters: MAKTOUB= It's written!!

AS AN AFTERWORD

(From Mr. Giannis' diary)

Midnight Saturday 25 to 26 September 201...

Tonight I drag my footsteps into the blessed cave, where You, my Lord, made your presence visible to Thy beloved student, to shed light on the elusive lust of this small great world.

Unworthy and humble me, I have eyes dejected to the ground, because I dare not face Your greatness and ask for Your mercy. Because that's how they taught me to do... How strange I feel, suddenly.

Your hand on my shoulder and Your presence next to me, as a bosom friend, ready to listen to me and support me.

For years, I've kept the flame that burned me deep inside. That fairy tale from the East, which told about the human souls who turn into singing flowers, what has become of it? How much I loved it! But the dream lasted for a while... and I, a little child, was left to look at its sad remains, as it was buried under tons of ash and boring "decent" sounds!

Oh, what I used to say every time to my students: "the real music, my children, doesn't need music or notes. It's deep inside us! A stimulus... a moment... and comes out like a precipitate river. And alas to the one who won't follow the voice of his heart! He will be doomed to drown in a shallow and meaningless life!".

Words... words... words! Hoping to have time to teach them at least that the price of betrayed dreams is high. My hair's been grayed.

Until the old forgotten fairy tale suddenly came alive.

The flower...

The scent...

The light...

The song...

The revelation of a painful truth...

The solution of a killing...

The redemption...

I left aside the music books and the notes...

The timbale was calling me from the depths of the desert, which talks about the princess of the East and the singing flower...

The gypsy's violin was calling me, who roams the castle cities looking for his own dream...

You're the only one who understands me without judging me!

Everyone else turns their backs on me, thinks I'm crazy.

But I'm ready to take the big step, because I know well now that, when my heart will be free, it will really be chanting Your glory as it feels and knows.

Without music and notes anymore.

Without dull and "decent" sounds.

The bird's singing can be enough..

The rustling of a flower...

The smile of a child...

The rain drops...

The stars in the desert sky...

The sound of a Gypsy violin...

That way I'll see You more clearly!!

Slowly, dawn is appearing.

For the first time, perhaps since I was born, I feel the need to sing loudly.

Everything around me an endless blue!!

PART B'

The Dance of Ayse

Room 25 at 'King Faruk' foundation, next to the banks of the Nile, on the island of Gezira, was like an artist's luxury dressing room. Red velvet curtains covered the windows while on the walls were photos of belly dance performances, film posters and newspaper clippings belonging to another era.
Next to the window, a woman immobile in a wheelchair was sitting and gazing the river hour after hour.

Even though she was over 50, her face was still keeping some youth and freshness. The black coll [1], which she applied on the eyelashes, further highlighted her dark amber eyes. Her black long hair, with a few gray hairs, was in a ponytail and hanging to the side.

She always wore red tight dresses, embroidered with beads, silk and silver.

She was rarely visited. The only people who entered her room were the doctor and nurse who took care of her. With the rest of the institution's patients she was friendly, but at the same time somewhat distant. She could talk about anything but herself. Several things on her were puzzling, but everyone respected and appreciated sayeda [2] Ayse, as they called her.

*****

---

[1] Coll=kind of mascara for the eyelashes

[2] sayeda= lady

That cloudy afternoon of September, the nurse who took her tea, noticed that Ayse was quite melancholic and cheerless. At other times she was welcoming her smiling, staring at her eyes and telling her thank you with her warm voice. Today, however, she seemed that she was unaware of her presence.

Worried, she approached the woman and put her hand on her shoulder.

"Is there something wrong, sayeda? Are you all right?" she asked her worrying.

Ayse nodded.

"Nothing's wrong, I'm fine," she whispered. *"Would you like me to keep you company?" "No, dear, I'd rather be alone! Go now!"*

She turned her eyes back on the Nile until she heard her room door shut.

From afar, the voice of the muezzin was heard from the mosque calling people for the evening prayer.

Ayse's look hardened, her lips started to tremble.

"At a day like today I lost everything! How many times I've asked you to save me from this hell!" she mumbled. *"How many times I prayed, I cried, I asked you to stand on my feet again! Fifteen years now the same prayer, the same tears... but nothing!"*

Old, faded images from the past started popping out in front of her.

*****

The woman with the sinuous body! The goddess of beauty! The symbol of love!

It was just a few of the big headlines that the newspapers and magazines were dedicating to Ayse Misir, one of the best belly dancers Egypt had ever known.

"Dancing is my life! Even when my time has come, I will do it by dancing!" she stated wherever she was.

From the cafes of Muhammad Ali Street, where all kinds of musicians, singers and dancers roamed, to the big hotels and nightclubs of Cairo, such as the *"Red Lotus"*, she had come a long way that had thrown her to the top.

Next to her, always the person who discovered her and established her: the famous Camellia el Maz, a true expert of the Eastern dances.

Their night performances at *"Red Lotus"* excited the crowds.

Fire woman Ayse was called by her fans, not only because of her wonderful dance, but also for the amazing costumes she was wearing.

Red all having the color of fire!

On the contrary, Camelia el Maz was wearing blue costumes and she always had a white silk scarf wrapped around her waist embroidered with beads.

How long does a dream last really?

A serious car accident changed Ayse's life forever.

The doctors fought by tooth and nail to save her from death.

But she would never walk again. How long does a dream last really?

She had handed over her place to a body stuck in the wheelchair and to a soul torn apart.

"Why did they save me, why?" she used to say in pain. *"I don't want to live like this!"*

She turned her eyes to the sky and asked to be relieved from that awful burden.

But she didn't get any answer.

"I want to stand on my feet! I want to dance again! Is it so much what I'm asking?" she was wondering through her sobbing.

*****

"You have a visit, sayenda!" the nurse's voice interrupted Ayse's thoughts.

Who remembered me? Almost everyone has forgotten me, they have buried me alive. Everyone, except her, she mulled.

"I don't want to see anyone!" she said trembling.

"Not even your old teacher and friend, Ayse?" a soft voice rang in her ears.

She turned towards the door astonished and saw a familiar tall and thin figure, dressed in blue, smiling at her.

"Camellia el Maz!" she only said.

Camellia el Maz entered the room, leaned and kissed Ayse on the cheek.

"I was afraid you had forgotten me! You haven't seen me in months!" Ayse said with a complaint when they were left alone.

"I never forget you, dear! I had to take a long journey, but now I'm back, near you!" Camellia reassured her.

They were silent for some time, each immersed in their own thoughts.

The sound of the rain drops interrupted their silence for a while.

"Remember? Once you and I used to tame the sounds of music. Now...nothing!" a sob cracked Ayse's voice.

Camellia got up and extended her hand towards her friend.

"Come dance with me!" she said.

"But, Camellia, I...! Don't you see me? Don't you see what I've become?"

"Everything is in your mind, Ayse! I know you can do it!" *"For God's sake, Camellia, why are you torturing me like that? It's been fifteen years since it's all over and you know it!"* *"Come on, Ayse!"* Camellia told her urgently, still having her hand extended towards her.

What if? Suddenly, a crazy hope crossed Ayse's mind.

She put her hands firmly on the cart's handles and tried to rise. Camellia grabbed her from her waist and helped her slowly stand up.

Ayse moved her feet with exertion while her friend was holding her firmly.

"You can do it, Ayse, you can do it! For so long you thought you couldn't, because fear held you back! You can do it!"

"Yes, I can!" Ayse repeated mesmerized.

Camellia gradually relaxed her hug. Ayse wobbled a little, but she didn't fall.

She took a few uncertain steps with her hands spread out. *"Come dance like before! Let go at the sound of music!"* Camellia said.

"But, I don't hear anything!"

"The music is in you, Ayse, in your soul and in your heart. Listen to it and let it lead you! You can do it!"

Camellia took Ayse by the hand and started swaying to the sounds of an invisible music.

Ayse closed her eyes and followed her teacher's footsteps.

"You're right, I can hear the music, too!" she said.How light she felt all the sudden!

She raised her hands out gracefully, and started making some moves with her body and her hips, timid at first and more intensely afterwards.

The music was getting slower and slower... and slower... until there was a flute left that filled the atmosphere with a sound like that of snake-charmer. Immediately, Ayse changed her movements along with the change of mood, and then she started with a waving movement of her pelvis, which rang up on her chest and down again.

The flute gave way to the timbale. Ayse adjusted to the intense rhythm and continued dancing with intense movements, circular and on the side, with her hips.

The same wonderful dance! The same unforgettable duo that once swept Cairo's stages!

A strong flash lit their faces.

"You're glowing all over!" Ayse said to Camellia. *"You've never been more beautiful!"*

"You too! Remember, it's never too late to live the dream!" Camellia whispered touched with emotion.

Meanwhile the light was becoming more and more blinding until it covered both women.

*****

"How did that happen?!" screamed Dr. Rahmad., the director of the institution, seeing Ayse fallen on the floor without moving. *"Why didn't you take care of her? What were you thinking?"*

"But... but she wasn't alone..." the nurse who took care of her dared to say. *"An old friend of hers came to visit her and..."*
"What friend?" he cut her short.
"It was a tall, thin woman wearing a blue dress and a white scarf on the waist. She was amazingly alike to an old dancer, I think she was the one! I heard sayenda call her Camellia el Maz!"
"What are you saying?! That old dancer you say, Camellia el Maz, has been dead for eight months!"
"That is impossible! I saw her with my own eyes!"
Dr. Rahmad pushed the girl aside and leaned over the fallen woman trying to bring her round.
It was hopeless. Ayse was dead.
She had a frozen smile on her lips.
She was already traveling for the land of sounds and music, where she could dance free forever.

*****

In Room 25 of King Faruk's Foundation, Dr. Rahmad arranged the final details of the funeral of sayeda Ayse.
"She lived alone and left alone!" he mumbled secretly wiping a tear.
"But why don't you believe me? I'm telling you, I saw her friend!" the young nurse insisted, making one last attempt to convince him.
"Stop that fairy tale, you irresponsible creature!" he yelled at her.
The girl cringed in a corner and burst into sobbing.
Dr. Rahmad let his gaze float on the Nile's calm waters.
"Bon voyage, sayenda," he whispered.
At a corner of the room, there was a left-off white silk scarf that was embroidered with beads. Neither of them noticed it.

Return

It's a cloudy Saturday morning. The middle-aged man, sitting comfortably on his seat of the train car, was absent mindedly looking at the landscape outside. At some point, he put his hand in the inside pocket of his jacket and pulled out a folded, crumpled envelope.

His sister's last letter, about a month ago

.....Father has had some heart aches lately. We took him to the city hospital, even though he insisted that "it's nothing". The doctor told him to be careful! Last night, just before he fell asleep, he whispered your name "Stephanos", among other things.

And the telegram he received a few days ago...

How long was it, really, since the last time he saw the man who had brought him to life? The proud Giorgos Rodiris? Successful wine producer and wine merchant, he destined Stephanos to be his successor in the family business.

But the young man was being magnetized by the vastness of the sea.

Father and son had a serious fight. *"I have other dreams for my life ..."*
"Neither you consider... nor respect anything..."

How did all these years passed by... all these years of solitude? thinks Stephanos, tightening the papers in his hands.

The sea is a seducer, which kept him close to her, sucking almost all his youth. He often used to write letters to his family and sent them pictures and postcards from various ports. His mother and sister were communicating as much as they could with him. From his father's side, silence.

*"He never forgave me for this "mutiny", as he told me back then
..."*, Stephanos mumbles to himself as the train enters the station.
 His sister was waiting on the platform. They hugged up in tears,
without talking.
They even didn't talk during all the way home. Only when they
entered the big hall where the coffin was placed, Stephanos finally
broke his silence.
"I want to be alone with him ..." he only said.
"But, my brother..."
"I want to be alone with him..." he said again.
His sister touched him affectionately on the shoulder and then
went out, quietly closing the door. Stephanos flightily touched his
fingertips on the cold, chilled face of the dead.
"I came..." he whispered. "I am here. For years you've waited for a
word, a move from me! For years I've waited for a word, a move
from you! *How did you and I become strangers?* All the time… all the
time I kept thinking about you. Even when I traveled for months in
foreign waters... even when I cast anchor in Spain for the sake of
Marisol, the mermaid from Valencia... even when our son Jorge
was born. He looks like you, father. If only you knew how much he
looks like you...'
A sob drowned him. He fought to contain himself.
"Every moment ... in every sorrow and joy ... I brought you to my mind,"
he continued. "You know... in my office at our shipping company there's
your picture... and whenever… whenever I came home… I dreamed you
were waiting for me… to hug me... to give me your blessing...! I wanted
to come and find you... to give you my hand... but I was afraid...! I didn't...
didn't make it after all... didn't make it..."

"*It's time, my son!*" the priest's voice interrupted him.

Stephanos nodded slightly.

Silent, with a bowed head, he followed the funeral procession. In his mind, he kept thinking about what Jorge had told him at their last meeting.

"*If mother were alive, she would surely understand me...*"

A stubbing in his heart the loss of Marisol, as if it were only yesterday, even though it was so long ago. He never forgot her and didn't want to put another woman on his side.

"*I have my own dreams too, father. Try to understand me, please.*"

Be close to our child, stand by him and advise him. But let him open his wings, pave his own way! Marisol's last words suddenly came to his mind.

My Jorge, my boy, he thought, wiping his tears.

His only son's great love was the wine and the vineyards.

His mental journey was interrupted by the noise the dirt made as it was falling on the coffin.

He went closer and threw a flower into the newly-opened grave.

Giorgos Rodiris, it's like your soul is asking to find a way out through the grandson you never met, he said to himself. But yes, it will be what you dreamed of for me... through him... it is his path, his life... who am I to prevent him?

"*Stephanos, are you okay?*" his sister whispered to him, holding his hand.

He nodded "*yes*" with his head, lost in his thoughts.

In your place, that damn telegram...! But I... I... I have to catch up... to catch up, father...!

He had made his decision. The next day he'd be on a plane and he'd go to Valencia. He already felt like he was missing his son a lot. And he had so much to tell him.

Dreams lost in the dust

AFTERNOON. I'm home alone. I open the closet and I'm looking for something. In the first drawer on the left, a wooden, carved box. I open it. The smell of lavender is flooding the place, while in my ears sounds a soft voice, like a whisper.

"Dreams sometimes look like dried flowers imprisoned in the trunk of time..."

The old, yellowish diary of grandfather Konstandis awaits me patiently.

Dreams Journal, it says outside written in large print hand letters.

...I want to be a teacher. To teach the children of my country about the world beyond these forests... beyond these mountains, I read on the first page.

...my princess has turned our little warehouse into a studio. And there she sits and draws blue skies and blue seas. "Someday we'll have a trip to show me the sea, eh, brother?" she tells me, hugging me tenderly. Yesterday she hanged a meadow full of red poppies in the big room... I read somewhere else.

Only that the financial ruin and the death of his father, made him change his mind. And one autumn morning he left for a trip beyond the forests and mountains of his country... for a trip to the great, vast sea.

October 20, 1920

Standing on the deck of the ocean liner, the first image I see is a tall, butch woman holding something like a torch in the hand, at the port entrance. Oh, yes, it's "The Statue of Liberty," which until recently I only saw in the School books. How far away that time seems to me now.

November 10, 1920

I have to catch the thread of my life all over again. Just give me strength, God!

December 1, 1920

It's cold. It's snowing. I put aside the coal shovel and rub my hands in a desperate attempt to warm them up. It takes a lot of coal to move the trains. We work long hours. When my shift finally ends and I return to my little room, I'm full of culm...
[.....................]

April 5, 1921

I raise my head up, in case I discover even one tiny bit of sky between the rumbling of the highway and the high, multi-storey buildings. I'm traveling with my mind. Mother will now be preparing the lunch table... my sister will be watering our rose bushes. The house... the yard... floodlighted in the sun.
[.......................................]

October 5, 1924

Today I sent a check to my mother at home. With this money, she's gonna get wheat and corn to sow in our field. I also told her to buy some green silk fathoms and sew a nice dress for my sister. My princess, my Smaragdi. I'm looking at her picture on my table and I smile. As time passes, she becomes more beautiful. Her hair, brown and curly, goes all the way down to her waist. Her eyes, blue-green, will certainly capture many hearts. Let mother not worry about the dowry of our Smaragdi. God bless my arms. I'll dower her well. But... but I want my sister to love and be loved. To live happily in a house full of sun, love and smile... to paint sunflowers... they will have the shape of the children she will bring to the world.

[.........................]

May 3, 1925

I got a letter from the village today. I bring it close to my nose and smell the air of the mountain and the pine. But it will have to wait, because now I have to go to work. It's almost midnight when I finally got back to my room. I can't stand of my feet from all the tiredness. Before I go to sleep, I want to read the mother's letter. Her words, even on paper, will rest me, lull me. I light the oil lamp, sit on the bed, open the envelope, and... No, it's not possible. My eyes are definitely fooling me. I'm rereading out loud, almost shouting, to realize that our Smaragdi is no longer be... I went to pieces. I fell down on my knees. Why, God, why?

[.................]

September 25, 1925

Stathios, the village daft. Daft and evil, cursed the moment he came to the world, the bastard. He dared to raise his eyes upon our Smaragdi. He lay in ambush when she was coming back from the field and... My Smaragdi couldn't bear the shame. They found her the next day hung in the barn. The shame is his, my angel, my flower and my gem. I came back with shattered wings. My angel, our angel, had gone forever. She wanted to live, to love and be loved, to paint suns, seas and poppies. Now... nothing anymore. They told me Stathios didn't mean to, that his mind was unsound. Words... words... words... He killed her. It was his fault. His... his... his...

[.....................]

I traveled alone beyond the sea in the hope of building new dreams. And when I came, I buried the dreams my princess didn't have time to taste.

[.....................]

NIGHT TIME. With my eyes wet, I close the last page of grandfather Konstandis' diary. The continuation of the story? Stathios the daft was found drowned in the river the night of September 25th to September 26th, 1925.

"He must have gone out to see the fairies naked... and they drowned him in the waters of the river... he was frivolous the poor soul."... some of the words spoken. But now I know...

A truth hidden in an old diary and in the bottomless depths of the heart.

I'm sure also some others back then suspected... they understood... but they never talked, because –maybe- that's how it should be done!

Grandfather Konstandis, faithful to the oath he made, got rid of Stathios, the man who became the cause of his sister ending her own life.

He lived with that secret...

Only just before closing his eyes, he confessed it to his son, Father-George, so that with a light soul could go to meet his Smaragdi.

I raise my eyes to the sky as the first light of the dawn rises. An invisible hand touches my shoulder.

"Dreams sometimes resemble to dried flowers locked up in the trunk of time... they wait for the moment we bring them to light."... and again this same voice.

In the meadow of red poppies hanging on my living room wall, a girl in a green silk dress, blue-green eyes and long curly brown hair waves at me, smiles at me, and then she fades away up high, curled up in the sun light.

A Sea of Memories

"Sea to drink you from the glass
in your blue waters to be lost
your body... I ask for your soul."

This was our song, the song of a love that marked my life beyond space and time. I wrote it for her when I was still a kid.

"Hey, Stelios, my son," Captain George's voice distracts me from my thoughts.

I'm turning towards him.

"I'm taking those foreigners with the boat across at Sapienza, to the golden beach! Do you want to come?"

I pause, and I can barely restrain a tear ready to roll on my cheek.

"Come on, my boy," the captain insists. *"Let's remember the old days... when you were little and I took you with me to throw the nets..."*

I'm ready to tell him that I don't want to let the pain nest in my soul or remember all the things that made me cry so much. Yet...

"I'm coming," I hear myself saying.

And now, as I'm sitting on the bow of the boat, my body is here, but my mind travels back in the past, to her.

How many memories, my God, how many memories!!

****

There was no sweeter creature in all of Methoni other than Captain George's only daughter, Rubi. Dark-skinned, with long wavy hair, almond-shaped eyes and a permanent smile on her mouth, she was for me the most beautiful dream, the love of my life. For her I was her baby, the little brother, as she precisely called me.

We had grown up in the same neighborhood, in Geranopolis, right next to the waves, and many of times we went together for swimming or escorted her father while fishing. On the island of Sapienza, on 'our island', as we called it, we had our first dreams, we sang our first songs, we played with water, we sat under the trees of the forest, and she would hug me, lulled me and told me stories about dragons, about princes and princesses and about countries far away.

"Would you like to see other places, Rubi?" I was worryingly asking her.

"Above all, I love our place..." she replied to me.

"I'm afraid."

"What are you afraid of, honey?"

"You may leave one day. A handsome prince will come and take you away from me! You'll forget me!"

"No...no! I will not abandon you, my angel," she used to say and kissed my eyes, to reassure me.

Oh, that kiss was sweeter than honey and I begged never to end! But life had other plans!

When I was finishing my first grade in high school, Rubi was leaving to study in Athens. The captain himself came to announce us the good news.

"Rubi succeeded at Training College with a top mark," he proudly said. My mother brought a morello cherry sweet to treat and wish for her.

"Your daughter is always worthy, Captain George," she said, smiling.

"We'll have the most beautiful teacher!" my father added. I couldn't talk! I felt like a witch had stolen my voice. I was very happy about Rubi, but this separation frightened me.

"Bravo for Rubi, Captain," I managed to utter.

"Are you sad that your childhood friend is leaving, son?" he kindly asked me.

I nodded *"yes"* with the head.

"Go find her! She's waiting for you down at quay!"

It was like I grew wings on my feet and ran near her. She was sitting on a little rock and she was looking at the sea, as if she was waiting for the boat that was coming to take her. The sea breeze waved her hair.

I approached her and I fell into her arms, crying.

"I love you," I told her softly in the ear. *"I love you..."*

"I love you too, little one," she replied, and she stroked my head, as if she would with a baby.

I looked at her almost desperately! I loved her so much. Nights and nights I dreamed of her, I wanted to touch her, to kiss her, make her mine, only mine, but she was now ready to open her wings and fly. Nothing and no one was going to stop her, so I, too, sealed my love to the bottom of my heart and silenced.

So Rubi left, leaving me as a farewell gift a silver little crucifix she had since she was a little girl and had never took off until the moment she gave it to me.

"To think of me while I'm gone, little one, and to feel me close to you," she told me hanging it on my neck.

In the hours I was alone, I brought it to my lips and kissed it with worship.

"Darling, you, my sea, don't forget me," I was whispering. Her two years of study passed fast like water. During holidays she always came to Methoni, close to us, but she was starting to change. She was prettier now, full of grace and self-confidence, and I felt so clumsy and so 'little' next to her. There was only one way to prove to her that I deserved her love.

"I'm going to study a lot, I'm going to be the best student and when I'm done with school I'm going to marry her!" I said stubbornly and I threw myself into the study.

"I will open the best store here in Methoni and treat her as a queen!! In summer afternoons we will be going to our island and..." I closed my eyes and imagined us swimming naked... the two of us... *"and then in the woods, under the trees ... my hands touching her breasts ... to kiss her greedily and avidly"*... I brought to my mind her kiss just before we parted over and over again. A tender kiss on the cheek... for me it was as if I had tasted the honey of the whole world.

Dreams I shared only with myself, in the cold nights of winter, as I waited for the summer to come.

For how long can a dream last?

Life had other plans!

Shortly after her graduation, Rubi was appointed as a teacher, but not at our land, but far away, somewhere in a village in Crete.

I felt like crumbling to pieces. I was melancholic, I didn't want to eat or drink, I wasn't talking to anyone.

"It's just teenager's phase, it's going to pass!" my parents were saying, ignorant of the chips I'd been going through.

The little crucifix she had given me as a gift, I took it off my neck and threw it in a drawer. I didn't want anything reminding me of her...

She refused me, she forgot me, I was thinking.

I finished high school and I still didn't know what I wanted to do in my life. Rubi was still living in Crete. It looked like she was happy there. I was learning news from her, of course, from Captain George, although nothing was the same anymore. I continued having some hidden hopes for us, but...

"My Rubi is getting married," her father told us one Sunday after church.

"How? When?" I asked him astonished.

Captain George laughed.

"Time flies, son," he said. *"You see... one of her colleagues loved her and asked me for her hand in marriage."*

"And you... did you agree, Captain?"

"Of course! He's a good man and he loves her very much. They'll be happy together."

Is it possible that he loves her as much as I do? What about her? I wondered.

"I wish... I wish her all the best..." The same night I was hard on myself.

"Fool!!!" I repeated over and over again as I was standing in front of the mirror. "How could you believe that Rubi would ever care about you? Wake up, finally, wake up! Now that she is about to begin a new life, do you think she'll have the time or the mood to think about you?"

After having spent many sleepless nights, I thought a lot, and finally decided — *did I maybe have another choice?* — to leave behind the world of shadow and dreams and try to find my own way.

My land was chocking me, I didn't fit in it anymore. I wanted to go away, make a fresh start.

My uncle's proposal, who had gone to seek for a new life in England, came at the right time...

So I began to set up my life on another land... and there I made roots.

Time passed. I had several relationships, but I didn't love anyone as much as Rubi. I continued to carry her inside me, keeping her secured in a corner of my heart as the most precious stone. Although I had come to terms with the probability of never seeing her again, sometimes, under the permanently cloudy sky of London, images of the golden beach and the forest of our island came to my mind and reality was once again tangled with the dream.

Until a letter brought me back after 15 years of absence.

****

"We're here!" Captain George's voice brought me back to today...

"Nothing has changed," I told myself as I set foot on the island's soil. *"Everything is as it was back then: the beach, the forest... everything is here!"*

"All but her!" the captain whispers.

"Tell me, Captain, what exactly happened?" I ask him. *"Her daughter, her pride! She was her one and only princess and she lost her! Her heart*

was broken, my Stelios! How much could she take? She's gone, my Rubi flew high up! It's just that..."

"What?"

"Just before she died... she asked for you..."

"She asked for me? Me?"

"She said... she said... "I love you, my little Stelios, my little brother.".. a tear ran down Captain George's eyes.

I bowed the head. A sob got out of my chest, then another one, until I started crying with sobs.

"Oh, Rubi, my soul! Why? Why?"

The captain's firm hand touched my shoulder.

"Courage, my boy, try to be strong!"

"I can't! I can't!"

"Look at me, son!!", he shouted shaking me up hard. *"Rubi was my only daughter, she was my everything! And yet, I didn't fall to pieces. I kept on living, I kept going... I kept going!!..."*

"Only... only God knows how much I suffer inside me..." he lowered the tone of his voice.

I raised my head and looked at him with a blurry look from all the crying.

"And the... the other one?" I mumbled with difficulty.

Even after all these years, I couldn't say her husband.

"I don't know! He disappeared...never gave any signs of life!"

"Could he still remember her?"

"Maybe!"

I made a move with my hand.

"I want to be left alone for a while. To remember... to relive..."

I moved forward inside the forest with trembling steps, where Rubi and I used to sit and she was telling me fairy tales, embraced me, kissed me on the eyes, lulled me...

"Where are you now, my sweetheart?" I asked myself. *"Ah, if only you could be here to hug me again as before... to flood me in kisses... to lull me... I need it so much...!!"*

I hid my face in my hands while tears ran down abundantly.

Suddenly I felt a warm caress in my hair and a soft voice whispering to me...

"Don't cry, my dear!"

I jumped on my feet, shaking. And then I saw her in front of me: sweet, cute, dressed in white, looking at me with tenderness.

"Rubi..." I managed to utter. *"Are you... are you here, then?"*

"I live in your soul, in your heart, in the air that you breathe," she responded to me. *"Relax, my eyes, my little one! I was waiting for you... you came!"*

I laid my hands towards her.

"I love you...don't go...stay with me," I begged her.

"But I'm with you. As long as you carry me inside, I will never die."

"I need you...next to me..."

"As long as you carry me in you, I will never die."

"Never stop loving me... Rubi."

I fell down unconscious. I woke up much later, on the boat that had, in the meantime, taken the way back.

"Are you all right, my son?" Captain George asked me worryingly.

"Yes, Captain, don't worry."

I let my gaze wander far away. The island had become a small dot on the horizon and was slowly fading away. But it would always be there waiting for me... it would always be my island.

I looked at the sun that was setting filling the sky with purple colors, and I saw again her shape smiling at me and waving her hand.

Spontaneously, the old, favorite song came to my lips:

> *"Sea to drink you from the glass*
> *in your blue waters to be lost*
> *your body... I ask for your soul."*

Goodbye, my darling, my one and only wonderful love, I thought clasping in my hands the little silver crucifix, slightly blackened by time, which I had found in the drawer of my old room in my home. My heart was calm, peaceful and, above all, full of her.

Last Melody

A ray of light manages to penetrate through the blinds. Surely, the sun will have risen by now. I get up out of bed slowly and open the window which overlooks the street. I've been feeling pretty tired lately.

I look up, just in case I make out a single little blue tint.

What do you expect to see, really? I wonder.

A little bit of sky... a little bit of sky, I hear myself saying.

I take a look at the calendar hanging on the wall of my chamber.

I faintly smile.

This day... last year... I'm telling myself.

Yes, today is not a day like the others.

A thought that comes to my mind makes me blush.

I open the heavily carved closet-remnant from other times-which is *'anxious to breathe'*, crammed between the bed and the bedroom door.

I put my hand among the dark-colored hanging clothes and take out a long, silk dress, with lace on the sleeves and the bosom, in a dark-blue color. With slow, almost ritual movements, I let it slip on me.

I look at myself in the mirror.

It is as if a magic wand stops time and in place of the old idol with the sad gaze, is Evanthia, the only daughter of lord Sarris, from Patmos, who dreamed of a life full of vast blue.

Evanthia... the only daughter of lord Sarris... I... with the hidden yearning in the chest, which was no other than Aggelis, the violinist.

I first saw him at the fair of Theologos, playing music and singing about love and passion, seas and mistrals. On 8 May, when the roses, the honeysuckle and the bougainvilleas were in their glory.

I was leading the dance, begging the Saint whose name was celebrated to help me steal a look from Aggelis. It was as if the skies were open that night.

"We talked" to each other with our eyes. And we said a lot. And in a hot afternoon, we exchanged our first kiss at the quay. Just before he left the island, he hung on my neck a locket with a blue stone which had the shape of heart.

I'll wait for you... I'll wait for you... I repeated inside me many times as the ship was leaving the harbor.

But he never came back. As if the sea had swallowed him.

In the months and years that passed, I was unable to find out any news about him.

As if he never existed.

Only in the fourth dream.

I once heard that there is no greater pain than the pain of shattered dreams...

You can't mourn for a lifetime a love that lasted as much as the blink of an eyelid!!!!

The voice of reason. A bitter truth. Blond Evanthia, the island girl, made way for Mrs. Evi, the wife of a major merchant. In a penthouse of a chic (I always hated this word, but...) region in Athens, I pretended to live. My consolation was the pots full of jasmine on my balcony, to remind me of that May...

A turbulent sea was my life...

And I recited at a small semi-basement apartment after the financial ruin and his death... my husband's.

Alone... counting the fake years I lived by his side... the fake life...

Only that little oasis, hidden in a corner of the heart, gave me strength and courage.

Every year, on this day, I put on the blue silk dress I was wearing back then… I hang the favorite locket on my neck… and let myself to travel and dream. These hours are only mine… I feel him close to me holding me tight, whispering sweetly… tenderly… singing to me.

But today, now, my strength is leaving me. The naughty beating of the heart is left to remind me of the once-brainless, romantic girl... I close my eyes. I hear music... the most wonderful music!

> *"Take me blue sea*
> *in the arms of my beloved, take me.*
> *Blow wind, blow the sails*
> *to find myself near her as soon as possible..."*

Oh, yes... it's the song he played, when I first saw him… I hear voices... a lot of voices... *"Mrs. Evi! Mrs. Evi!"*

Someone's shaking me.

But I'm no longer here, I'm traveling to the sounds of this last melody. My only luggage a kiss and a locket. I don't need anything else.

When the almonds bloom

He was told clearly. There was no more hope, no more return. And he bent his head so as not to show the tears he was painstakingly holding back. So that's it. Winters and summers would pass, spring would come, and he would still remain nailed there, unable to walk, to run, to talk, to breathe deeply.

For a long time now he is in the same position and his whole world is a room, a bed and a box! A wooden box full of envelopes, others large others small, with a common feature: all coming from the same person.. the girl with the brown eyes, the sweet smile and the difficult name. His tongue, which no longer made sounds, was confused when he was trying to pronounce it. That's what he called her Blue, because she came from the land where the vast blue was ruling, a blue that God had spent so lavishly.

Her letters opened for him a window to the world... a world full of love, light and almond flowers. Between the words he was trying to hearken the beatings of her heart! At times, fear was biting his soul like a snake.

*Let her open her wings! The more you tie up with her, the harder it will be later to...*Blue a blossoming flower... and he stuck on a chair, on a bed, with a damn machine measuring his breath! But she was his Blue, his own Blue.

Is it so much that I dream? he was thinking. I love her as much as she doesn't know and she might never know...

How much he longed to see her in front of him! Her eyes in his eyes, her hands in his hands! If only she could see what was going on inside him... and then... Damn disease!

The people around him were trying to bring him down to earth.
 Don't hold her! Let her open her wings and fly.
Really, how can you shut in your hands the vast blue? But still,
without her, he'd feel half, he'd be half!

******

I'll come...
when your eyes become one with the sky
I'll come...
to teach you to speak the language of love
I'll come...
to join my heartbeat with yours
I'll come...
even when you're not waiting for me anymore
I'll come...
when the almond trees blossom...

Sweet words, soft, popping up from a piece of paper full of
smudges.
His Blue was writing beautiful lyrics! He imagined them dressed
in music, the most beautiful and sweet music. Maybe... maybe it
was a message from her which revealed...
If only...
Dreams...
When the almond trees blossom...
Oh, if only he could see her, feel her, even for one moment!

*Let her go! This love can't bear fruit! It can't... it can't! Weak
and nailed on a chair, you'll try later to pick up your pieces...*
How much he wanted to muffle that voice!!!

****

The days were passing and this song had stuck in his head for good.
A song, because, when he was listening to music on his old stereo
player — since he never wanted to be separated from his vinyl
records — he dressed it with the lyrics of his Blue.
 He had read them so many times that he had learned them by
heart. And the paper, apart from the smudges, it had marks of
kisses and tears.
The winter was about to end. Spring would be here soon. So what?
*Night and day, day and night he would be there, all alone. The only way
out was through her letters, her photos... until when really?*
The night had half passed, but he remained awake thinking...
How can you shut in your hands the vast blue?
A strange rustle made him jolt a bit... a touch...
He lit the lamp next to him.
And then he saw the vast blue sky closed in two eyes and a smile.
His Blue!
He tried to say something, forgetting for a moment that his voice
was long lost. She gently shut his lips with her hand.
I know, he heard her saying. *But your voice is here...* and she showed
up on his heart.
She caressed his face, his hair… she took him in her arms and let
him taste a sweet and deep kiss…

His heart started beating fast. But her kiss was not enough. He wanted to get lost inside her and suck up the almond scent she was emitting.

My soul, he felt all his being screaming, as his Blue, having been rid of her clothes, leaned on him and started kissing him everywhere. He was shaking all over! Time was lost! There were only two bodies, full of sweat and fire, dancing at the rhythm of love and sometimes dancing as calm as the raindrops and sometimes as vibrant as a rough sea.

I'm yours, make me your own... always the same cry. He saw thousands of stars shining in the vast sky and then falling, falling, falling.

When a star falls, you have to make a wish...so they say! My Blue... my almond... don't leave me... hold me... hold me...

He plunged his face into her naked breasts. She held him tight on her and whispered in his ear the one and only word he longed to hear.

My love...

Even if it was in a language he never spoke.

Tonight, he understood everything so clearly.

My love, he got lost again inside her.

****

It was around noon, when they found him sleeping with a picture while the forgotten needle was scratching the record on the stereo player. The blue box was capsized on the carpet… the sheets creasy and wet… in the air the strong scent of the almond blossoms.

He had forever plunged into the sea of her love. He opened his own wings, eventually, and traveled to where he could speak out loud, laugh, breathe freely. In a vast garden full of almond trees, he would wait for his Blue worshiping her for eternity.

*****

On the small island, the almond trees were in their prime... their flowers more beautiful than ever! The girl with the brown eyes and the sweet smile came out on the balcony to enjoy the beauty of the afternoon.

It was growing dusk. The sun was walking toward its set. In the distance of the horizon, the sky had taken a strange shape… Two big, sweet and expressive eyes that looked at her with all the worship of the world. The almond blossoms next to her moved vigorously. The soft breeze became a caress on her hair and face and a whisper in her ear.

Just one word: *My love!!!*

Flutter of Souls

Her name called to mind of sky and sea, waves and seagulls... her only company! For a long time now, Pelagia had settled her loneliness in a small house on the rocks, quite outside the thorp of the Arcion island. A small dot, in the vast blue sea, embracing the Dodecanese.

Dreamer and romantic, she didn't match her countrymen, who called her light-headed and shook their heads with pity whenever they saw her with that faded, old notebook in the hand writing... and writing... and writing...

"Poor one!" they whispered allegedly compassionately. Perhaps inwardly they were jealous of what they themselves did not have or dared to have: the strength to be able to dream and fill a page only with the whole world's beauties, colors and scents.

But Pelagia didn't care! She preferred the world of dreams to the daily round that the people around her were experiencing. In this way, she enjoyed the sunrise and sunset, whose presence was overhanging royally over the Aegean or she got lost for hours in the cave at the bottom of the rocks, the fairy cave, as they called it. It was connected to an old legend that had passed as a fairy tale from generation to generation. At many winter nights, when the raindrops were rhythmically hitting the roofs of the houses, grandmothers were talking about the gorgeous fairy whose beauty stole the heart of the young prince. A great love was born, but it wasn't meant to be settled. He was killed in the war, leaving his beloved disconsolate. Night after night her painful mourning was heard. Her soul was captured by pain. The tears clouded her bright eyes, her beauty withered. She withdrew deep into the cave and never appeared again in the sunlight.

Fear had overwhelmed the inhabitants of the island, that is why no one ever headed there, except for the *"poor, light-headed woman who talked to herself!!!"*.

In Pelagia's hermitage, after all, only the seagulls and waves could hear her voice. And it was the silent voice of an unspent love, asking for a way out to light to live.

The photo, slightly wrinkled from the moisture, which she discovered by chance one day at the entrance of the fairy cave (unknown and strange how it had been found there!), had become her whole world. The dark male figure with the honey eyes greeted her silently in the mornings and said good night at nights. And she was talking to him, smiling at him... a thousand-of-a-word feelings overwhelmed her heart, but also the time-worn notebook where she was depositing her inner feelings.

You're far from me...I never met you, and yet I loved you a photo only...and all my thoughts about you on a piece of paper...

You look like an angel dressed in white a grief hidden in your eyes you try to fool it behind a smile. You're far from me...I never met you and yet I hearken your breath, your heart, your voice.

Just for a moment...
let me reach out and touch you
bring you under my sky
under my own sun
on blue coasts
naked to swim in crystal clear waters...
and at nights
when the moon light will fall softly to whisper you sweetly and
tenderly
just one word: MY LOVE.

Words full of love, full of sea and saltiness that come from the yellowish pages, they fly... fly and arrive in a country far away, full of strange colors and scents.

The man in the photo, with the sweet smile and the gloomy look, was looking out of his window at the city lights. The thoughts in his head had staged a wild dance, since for some time now a strange dream had haunted his existence: scenes from a place full of wild beauty, rocks and sea all around... and the figure of a woman who was one with the vast blue!! He'd never seen her before, but she was so familiar to him. At nights, he was dragged with her into a wild, intoxicating, love game. The words coming out of his mouth were in a language unknown, that he had never spoken before. Love and desire had taken him over for a vision. But who would he talk to about what was happening to him? No one would believe him and they would laugh at him for sure. So he was sitting down writing letters having as a recipient this unknown beloved, which remained locked in his drawer. Like tonight, when his hand, as if it was driven by some invisible force, began to carve words...

It is enough I know you exist... In your dreams I will join you until the moment I meet your soul in the land where music never stops. Tonight I dreamt of you...

You came like a vision at my bedside, the moment when fever made me delirious in a language I had never spoken before. How tired I am of the gods I've loved for years... the secret-sacrifice flames I've lit...

When I saw you becoming one with the fire and the sea, I realized how futile everything was.

I touched my hand trembling on your chest

My eyes stuck THERE...

You caressed my forehead...

You took out the cross you were wearing and you put it in my palm kissing it gently.

"It will keep you forever safe," you whispered to me.

"Stay," I tried to yell at you, but you had already gone in the fog.

I opened my eyes...

In my hands, trapped was your amulet.

A tear has fallen from my eyes

A word came out of my lips in that language I had never spoken before

Just one word

MY LOVE.

This night, he felt as close to her as ever.

He lifted his eyes off the paper.

Half of the night had passed, but he kept being awake, dreaming and writing...

I kept your amulet in the palm and kissed it it looks like the sweetness of your lips... I hung it over my chest and since then, I've been counting your heartbeats... and I dream of blue sea and sky blue sky and sea... the spell of your land I desired...naked to swim with you in crystal clear waters making love to you into magic caves holding you in my arms until dawn... with you counting the alphabet of stars... with you hearkening the sounds of the violin in the night's silence...

The first rays of the sun found him sitting in the same position. He wasn't alone, some were talking to him, they were nudging him, but he was traveling...

I travel... I travel... I travel

My soul is filled with blue sea and sky blue sky and sea...

The world around me just a vast blue.

Pelagia woke up with a strong feeling. As the first light was beginning to dawn, a beautiful flower came and landed next to her. Its color red as the passion, its scent intoxicating like the scents of a dream land. And when she took it gently in her hands, she felt a whisper...

The vast blue of the sky and the sea

I crossed to find you...

My soul, a flying bird, my body a flower... and a scent the words of the heart in the language I had never spoken before...

I don't need anything else but this word: MY LOVE!!!

Uncomprehending, she looked at the photo of the one who had captured all of her being. It's as if she'd seen him smile at her, sweeter and more tender than ever. Almost shaking, she left a kiss on the paper where his lips were.

"You're here!" she only said.

Suddenly, the window opened with a big bang and a strong current of wind grabbed the picture from her hands. No... no... it can't be... it can't be... she thought.

She jumped out of the covers and dashed outside, shouting *"MY LOVE!!!!!!!"* many times. Her soles were grazed by the gravel and bled, leaving red tracks on the path, the sweat made her nightgown stick to her body, but she didn't care. She kept running and shouting.

A fisherman who had come out on his boat off the coast saw her from afar and crossed himself.

"There goes the poor one, she lost it completely!" he said.

With misty eyes, tired-out, Pelagia sat on a rock. That's it.

Now... nothing, she thought.

She looked far away towards the thorp. In fact, it had never been her land though she grew up there. She was a foreign body... crazy, light-headed, fairy-tale like... oh, yes, she knew their rue very well.

At her feet, the sea, crystal clear and blue, seemed to open her its arms.

She didn't hesitate for a second...

She dived into the water and sucked in the saltiness, letting it pass through every bit of her body. She swam slowly, until she got to where it all started, in the fairy cave.

"Here I will wait for you, here, for as long as it takes!" she said quietly. *"Like she did... back then..."*

An invisible hand grabbed her gently from the shoulder and started pushing her inside the cave. A caress in her hair and a whispering female voice "Don't be afraid! Come on!" made her let go with trust.

She walked... walked... walked... she lost track of time. The deeper she went, the more intense the smell of exotic flowers around her became. Sweet music sounds resonated everywhere.

And then she saw him...

Sitting on a rock, he was waiting for her...

"Welcome, daughter of the sea, my eternal one and only beloved!" he said, closing her in his arms.

"If only you knew..."

"I know! Now we'll be together forever! You and me... in the land where music never stops!"

He kissed her many times, on the eyes, on the lips, on the neck, and then he led her into the dance steps...

Hidden behind a thick tree trunk, the cave fairy smiled for the first time after centuries of pain and tears. The gorgeous beauty of her face may have withered, but she never lost the beauty of her soul. The moment of her freedom had come! She sent a kiss to the dancing couple and then she flew up high. It was time to meet her own destiny.

Pelagia didn't appear on the island again. For a long time, the locals speculated about the disappearance of the light-headed, and whenever their road led them near the area where she lived, they crossed themselves and touched wood as no evil could come to them!

One thing was for sure: she in a world of dreams found the happiness she didn't taste in the world of humans.

Pelagia's old notebook and the letters of the man with the honey eyes are kept in a safe place. Maybe someday they'll help the fluttering of some other souls on the path of love.

The most beautiful things can be seen only with the eyes of the heart.

The Tale of Shehrazade

For some time now, the dawn light was struggling with the darkness of the night over the sacred island. In the town, where the Monastery of Theologos overhangs it, only the blow of the wind was heard. There was silence everywhere.

In the ledger, two three vigil candles lit up the icons with their shimmering light, giving out a bizarre majesty, but sweetness at the same time, in the figures of saints.

Brother David came down carefully, quietly almost, the stone steps leading to the temple. He respectfully crossed himself, he asked for repentance, and then he withdrew into a dark corner, he bent his head and started praying.

"Give him strength, Lord," he murmured. *"And to me! Redeem me..."*
With trembling lips, he started reciting quietly... Have mercy on me God at your great mercy, and in the crowds of your settlements eradicate my every guilty act...

Despite the winter cold, he felt his forehead and palms sweating. For the most part, wash me out of my lawlessness and my sin, cleaning me up. That I'm aware of my sin and my sin before me is once and for all, he went on, trying to contain the shaking of his hands.

Behold if you're unlawfully arrested...

A slight sound of steps made him turn his head suddenly. *"Sorry...your blessings,"* heard a voice *"The Lord..."* David replied.

The young man shyly approached the monk.

"I didn't want to disturb the hours of peace..." he said again, but David cut him off with a nod.

"Don't apologize!" he said. *"Be blessed."*

The young man mumbled a thank you and looked down.

"I... I felt lonely upstairs... and maybe here...", the sob that suddenly came out of him didn't let him go on. *"The faith... the prayer... for whatever you want..."*

"...to empty my soul is what I want... to send away this void I feel inside is what I want...", he showed with his hand the place of the heart.

David suddenly shriveled. He grabbed the lad's chin, making him lift his head. Their eyes crossed.

Is it possible? he thought.

For a week now, he's been discreetly watching the newly-comer maintainer for the icons of the Monastery. He was more or less 28 years old, tight-lipped and bashful, with a natural courtesy that won the others from the very first moment. But he sensed that he was hiding some kind of bitterness, some pain inside of him. A couple of nights some monks had heard him cry and talk like he had someone else in the cell with him.

His facial features, his movements, the tone of his voice, reminded something to David. And today he made sure, seeing that gardenia-shaped ring he was wearing.

"Everything ... everything can be cured ... there is the right medicine for everything, my boy ... for everything, my Lucas," he said.

Lucas (that was the young man's name) was swallowing. These words were coming out of the past.

"So, here again, after all this time..." he told him again and kissed him on the forehead.

"Almost a decade..." Lucas said. *"But how???"*

Actually, he didn't want anyone to recognize him. But now... How childish! he thought. Then how did he come to this place, where he experienced happiness and misery together... where his existence was marked... where his old teacher, Brother David, became a monk... *could he ever pass unnoticed by this man...?? "Only one person was wearing such a ring... she... and we both know it well..."*

How can time go back?

"Still you couldn't forget?" David asked him with compassion.

"I will never forget," Lucas replied.

"Never is a strong word... and you are still a child..."

"I'm no longer a child..."

"Whenever you want to talk..."

"I don't trust anyone anymore, master..." That's what he always called him: master.

Yesterday is tangled with today, today with yesterday, and Lucas feels like he is the 17-18 year old teenager again... the loner... the perhaps misunderstood.

The raindrops soaked his face and the tiles of the monastery's yard. Though David would swear that the drops in Lucas' eyes and cheeks were rain and tears together, tears and rain.

Lucas made a turnabout and headed to the lab, where the maintenance and restoration of any damage on the icons were done. Working would make him feel better. This had been going on for a long time now...

In the evening he alleged a headache and didn't come down for dinner. The abbot asked a monk to take him something to eat. Not a few minutes passed and the monk came back with a pasty face.

"Lu... Lucas..." his voice was trembling.
"Lucas... what?"
"With your permission, Superior, may I go to him?" David asked. *"He was an old student of mine... maybe I can..."* The abbot nodded affirmatively.

*****

Lucas' cell door was half open. David knocked discreetly and when he didn't get an answer, he pushed it gently and went in. And then he froze.
Over the bed, the eyes of the dark woman in the portrait met his. Her hair was falling softly on her shoulders, her expression was dreamy... and on her finger that gardenia-shaped ring... *"The... the..."* he couldn't continue.
"The one who taught me to dream..." Lucas whispered.
"Did you paint that?" David asked.
He suddenly grabbed him from the arm.
"How... where... when...???"
He believed that she had gone with the forgetful river, but here she was, coming back to life in front of him. For ten years he believed

that constant prayers had shielded him and now his 'armor' had cracked... again...

"I painted it... seeing her with the eyes of the heart... when..."

"You live... you live with a ghost..."

Lucas beckoned David to sit down while he pulled a little bottle of whiskey out of his bag and extended it to him. *"Drink, master..."* he told him.

"I..."

"Drink..." he said to him again, as if he almost ordered him. And as the dark veil of the night lay on the island, the time of confessions and revelations began.

"I learned next to her to spell the stars alphabet. On the nights of my solitude, her eyes popped up in front of me. Against those of you who could not or did not want to see... she opened the gateway that led to the world of the fairy tale and dream... and there I wanted to hide forever away from what hurt me. The name on her papers was lost in the fog of time... because from the first moment I saw her for me she was Shehrazade... my Shehrazade. How long does a fairy tale last, master? As long as the delicate fragrance of a dried gardenia that accompanies dreams forgotten in the trunk of time... dreams that gave meaning to my existence and kept me standing..."

While Lucas was talking, David traveled with the mind.

In a building with visible signs of fading glory...at the time his name was Peter, he had performed his theological studies in Athens and Istanbul and was appointed there on the holy island to convey morality first and foremost to his students.

"Severity! Severity is necessary!" the schoolmaster's words echoed sharply in his ears, that's how almost frowning he always entered the class.

The same was more or less what his other colleagues believed. Until she invaded everyone's life and his.

It was a creature that loved everything that had to do with colors and scents. Her smile was spreading warmth everywhere... you think she'd come to stir their stagnant waters...

"Behind the seemingly rebellious teenager, my Shehrazade distinguished what I was actually. A creature scared, immersed in solitude, without his own people to support and advise him. I was thirsty for love, and she opened the hydrants of her soul to quench my thirst... I thought everything around me was gray or black, and she pulled the heavy curtain that hid the world of colors from me. Her voice... her lips were dribbling oriental sherbet..."

This oriental sherbet, this sweetness, Peter, the strict theology professor, wanted to taste. The one who up until recently was living a monotonous life, being devoted to his teaching and research work and his mission of moral principles and untouched values, had begun to be overwhelmed by a wild passion for his colleague, Shehrazade, as it had finally prevailed by all to call her, since this woman loved fairy tales, but stressed that the most fascinating fairy tale is our own life.

"How much strength and courage I obtained. My life was flooded with color, smile and gardenia scent... filled my white painting block with

drawings... and my soul with various feelings... for me Shehrazade was everything... teacher, mother, friend, sister, lover... yes, master, lover. I loved her as much as nothing else in my life... with her I traveled the sea of love..."

Oh yes! In that sea where Peter was longing to travel with her, that young lad took his place!! *How could he forget?*

He remembers...

Finally, he had decided to visit her and talk to her about what he felt inside. And if she wanted...

It was nearly dusk when he arrived at her little house, in a lonely location, by the sea.

The curtains of the living room were half open… and that's how he saw them from the glass...

A cluster the naked bodies of Shehrazade and Lucas traveled together and through their moaning words were heard full of flame, words sweeter than honey.

An invisible force kept him there, stuck and he saw everything. All this time the couple's love encounter lasted he was biting his lips, he was clutching his fists so forcefully that they became white, while the blood was drained from his face, becoming at once a pale mask.

It was unfair! Very unfair! He stepped back, eventually, and he left like he was being chased. When he was far away, he kneeled to the ground and the cry that came out of him sounded loudly within the vastness of the Aegean.

David was shaking and had a good sip of whiskey from the bottle.

Oh, my God, why... why after all these years... *why..??* he thought. Lucas, lost in his confession, didn't notice.

"I know...it was incompatible...I was 18 and she had already been in her thirties!! Believe me, master, I loved her very much...even though my soul was dreading nothing to be revealed... not for me, but for her... I knew firsthand how cruel and merciless people can be..."

People can become cruel and merciless, especially when they get hurt, David thought.

Peter was intending to talk to the Principal and expose to him what he saw. But he never did. Could it be that the whispering comments behind his back held him back? The kind of *gossiping "what was he doing visiting her at night"?* But what he saw marked him intensely. So intensely... that he finally preferred to take things into his own hands.

"Who decided to put such an unexpected and unfair end to this fairytale? What cruel reality awakened me from the beautiful
dream I lived in? The sea full of blood... The blood of my Shehrazade... how much blood, my God, how much blood..."

He cut off his confession abruptly and covered the face in his palms. David, with a shaking hand, caressed his shoulder. *"My child!"* he only said.

The unexpected and tragic death of Shehrazade had upset everyone. Who could possibly hate her so much?

No one has ever been able to give an answer. So, little by little everything was covered up by the oblivion of time.

No one has been able to give an answer. Maybe except for one...
David closed his eyes, trying to relax his naughty heartbeat. Damn images, that thought he'd put them away for good, started pouring up in front of him. From back then... when he was still Peter...

****

For quite some time, Peter was hiding behind the bush, observed his fairy, who had dived all naked into the little bay. Oh, it wasn't fair to have another guy tasting her body, and especially that kid! He... he would make her his queen... he would give her everything... as long as she gave him a smile, a kiss...!!

He imagined her making love to him for hours and hours whispering in his ear the word *"I love you!!"*
His oppressed manhood, almost buried in volumes of dusty theological books, was desperately looking for a way out.

A few steps separated them. If only he could find the courage to hug her..He took a deep breath...Finally, show you are a man! he told himself. Shehrazade came out of the water. In her marmoreal body, the drops of the saltiness were shining, mixed with the colors of the nightfall. She wrapped the towel around her, when two hands grabbed her by the shoulders.

"My darling! My darling! My life!" crazy with lust Peter clasped her on him and kissed her on her lips, on her neck...
"Let me go...let me go, you're hurting me!" she yelled, trying to escape. She found the power to push him...

"Leave me..." she said to him again trying to cover her nudity. *"I couldn't hold myself...forgive me... I love you, my darling... if only you knew... how many nights I've spent awake... for a long time now... I want you... I love you... my soul.."*

The whole scene seemed rather funny. The severe theology professor Peter Harisis, on the ground, begging her, almost crying...

Without paying attention to him, she turned her back on him and started to dress up.

"You are everything for me... you... you..." he continued his delirium.

"Go, Peter, please," she said, making a great effort to keep her cool.

"You don't want me...you don't want me..." Peter cackled out of control. *"You prefer him... I saw you... I know everything! Tell me... is he better than me, huh? Is he better? What does he do to you in bed? What's he telling you? But... ha ha ha... I'll show you... what I can do... and you'll see... how beautiful it will be... ha ha ha ha ha."*

The strong slap Shehrazade gave him was the answer.

"Go... get out of my sight..." she yelled at him. *"Impotent... coward..."*

Impotent… coward... the words were like knives piercing his ears. He jumped on her like a vicious horse, threw her down and started hitting her.

"You like it like this, don't you? Is that what you like? Ha ha ha ha"

"You're not a man..."

How much he wanted to silence that voice. He mugged her mouth with one hand while he tried to lift her skirt with the other.

By making a superhuman effort, Shehrazade kicked him with the knee between the legs.

Screaming with pain, Peter rolled to the side.

"You're not a man, you..." she told him again.

He didn't realize how he grabbed the stone in his hands and started beating the girl on the head with frenzy.

"Shut up... shut up... shut up…" he shouted as he beat her up.

"You're not a man, you!!!" He thought he was listening over and over again...

Panting, all of a sweat, he stopped when he realized that Shehrazade was no longer moving. The blood had flooded her hair, her face, her body, and its color was mixing with the blue sea...

When he realized what he had done, he started to tremble. And now what???

***

"I KILLED HER!" David shouted. *"I DID...."*

"WHAT ARE YOU TELLING ME, MASTER?? YOU??? BUT HOW IS IT POSSIBLE?" Lucas couldn't believe what he was listening to.

"I.....ah, I… I… I… Peter Harisis the theology professor… I, brother David I'm a killer! Everything is pointless... all in vain..."

"You???? On whose shoulder I cried when she was found dead... and you were mourning with me... with all of us... you??????" Lucas was out of control.

He wanted to grab the monk-who was shaking like a leaf- in his hands and squeeze his throat but no... not yet.

*"How did you cover the tracks and no one suspected you? How??????
How?????"* he yelled shaking him from his shoulders.
"The darkness of the night... the darkness of the night and..." a strong
cough made David fold in two.

***

It was as if the damn luck had allied in favor of Peter. It was
precisely in those days that he received the avulsion he so wished
for and left to teach at the Patriarchal School in Istanbul.
But the remorse, along with the desperate love he felt, didn't let him
rest for a minute. So, looking for peace, he visited the Monastery of
the Holy Trinity in Halki for a while, and that's where he made the
decision to follow monk's life. Praying, fasting and repentance
would certainly calm his troubled soul.

Spirit crushed, heartbroken and tense, God will never exhaust...
He thought he had succeeded to some extent... even when he
returned to the sacred island, the island of the Apostles, at the
Monastery of Theologos. But nothing lasts forever, after all...

***

"Some water..." David begged Lucas. *"Please."*
The lad sighed deeply. He deprived him from the woman he loved,
condemning him to drag his pain and loneliness for years through
transient relationships, without being able to root anywhere. And
fate had saved him the toughest game for the end. Here he came,
hoping to finally exorcize his pain, with prayer and spiritual

guidance from his old teacher, he learned the hardest, the most painful truth.

"Some water..." David's voice sounded weak... the breath could not come out of his chest...

"She was so beautiful with her blue dress and the flowers in her hair! Except that she didn't talk to me... she didn't talk to me anymore! And I, with shaking hands, took the ring with the gardenia she was wearing... it became one with my finger... one with me from now on..."

He had a look full of pity and contempt to the man who was crawling at his feet.

"Good night, master!" he only said.

He went out. He wanted so much to breathe some fresh air. He stayed there until David's breath became a throes and his heart stopped beating.

He went inside, unslinged the portrait, took it in his arms and left without looking behind.

He started the engine of his car and drove... he drove... until he was there, in the little house by the sea, where he first met love. It was almost dawn.

As the sun began to rise at the bottom of the horizon, a gardenia scent flooded everything around it.

"I love you!!" he said out loud. *"Our story never ended, my life. Good morning, Shehrazade!"*

THE END